And Then It Happened
~13~

AND THEN IT HAPPENED

~~13~~

M & L Wade

Books for Boys

ISBN 9780988115231

Printed in Canada by Hignell Book Printing

Books For Boys Inc.
P.O. Box 87
Strathroy ON N7G 3J1

Table of Contents

Chapter 1

With Friends Like That

Have you ever read a book that completely changed your life? Yeah, me neither. But being best friends with Gordon can be life-changing enough every day. Even something as simple as going for a walk can suddenly turn into a life and death struggle. For example, one beautiful fall Saturday afternoon, Gordon, Paulo and I were out looking for empty cans and bottles that we could return for some easy money. We had walked quite a distance and our garbage bag was about half full. We were well outside of town, trudging down dirt roads, our eyes glued to the ditch, when suddenly Gordon stopped in his tracks.

"Did you hear that?" he said.

"Hear what?" I asked.

"That rustling and grunting noise that sounded like a bear."

"Everything in the woods beside a deserted dirt road sounds like a bear," said Paulo, barely looking up from the ditch in his search for empties. "It's probably just a mouse running through some dead leaves."

We continued on for a few seconds, and then I heard it, too. There *was* a rustling and grunting noise, and it was definitely coming from the woods.

"Sounds awfully big for a mouse," I said nervously. Then I got a whiff of something that didn't smell like a mouse, either. Just as I was about to ask if anyone else smelled something really bad, out from the woods came the biggest, meanest looking bear we'd ever seen! We froze!!

Fortunately, Gordon, Paulo and I had spent many hours discussing exactly what we'd do in such a situation. First, we would remain calm. Second, we would stick together. Third, we would calmly back away from the bear, keeping our eyes on him the whole time. It was a great plan, at least when we were sitting in the safety of our bedrooms or our treehouse. Here, in the middle of nowhere, on a lonely deserted dirt road, our plan suddenly seemed *insane.* Without so much as looking at each other, we immediately devised a new plan. First, we panicked. Second, we sprinted off in three different directions. Third, we climbed the closest trees we could find, sat on a branch, and closed our eyes, hoping that the bear wouldn't see us with our eyes tightly shut.

Apparently, the bear was familiar with this plan, and he calmly ambled over to Gordon's tree and began sniffing around the base of it. He stood up on his hind legs and eyed Gordon hungrily. Then he let out a loud grunt, licked his chops and began climbing up Gordon's tree! I sighed with relief, I mean sadness, and watched as the bear slowly made his way from branch to branch, getting closer to Gordon with each passing second. Saliva dripped from the bear's sharp fangs and I could see his huge claws digging deep into the bark as he made his way up the tree to his dinner. When the bear had nearly reached the branch Gordon was perched on, Gordon took off his running shoe and waved it at the bear.

"Here, bear!" he called. "Come and get it!"

Has Gordon gone mad?? I thought. *Why is he tempting the bear to come closer?*

The bear sniffed Gordon's running shoe, and then Gordon hurled the shoe with all his might and shouted, "Go get it!!"

The shoe flew through the air and landed at the base of *my* tree!

"Thanks a lot, Gordon!" I yelled.

Thinking that the shoe might taste better than Gordon, the bear climbed down the tree and lumbered over to investigate. He sniffed the shoe and pawed at it before deciding it really wasn't anything he wanted to eat, but then he caught sight of *me*, huddled nervously on a branch high above his head. The bear snorted and licked his chops again, and then he began climbing up *my* tree!!

In a flash I took off *my* shoe and hurled it towards Gordon's tree. In my terror, I threw the shoe too hard. It sailed past Gordon's tree and landed at the base of Paulo's tree. Paulo's face turned pale.

"Sorry," I said weakly. To my relief, the bear climbed down my tree and headed over to Paulo's tree. After sniffing my shoe, he noticed Paulo up in the tree, and just as the bear was about to climb up Paulo's tree, Paulo quickly threw one of his shoes towards Gordon's tree. For the next ten minutes, shoes, socks shorts and t-shirts were hurled at each other's trees until finally we were down to our underwear. If I weren't so scared, I would have found the scene very funny. The three of us were sitting in trees, nearly naked, while a huge hungry bear went from tree to tree, sniffing our clothes in search of something to eat. What would he do when we ran out of clothes? We were about to find out…

As the bear began climbing Gordon's tree again, Gordon had no choice but to take off his underwear and hurl them at Paulo's tree. They landed in a branch about halfway between Paulo and the ground. The bear was *very* interested in the underwear and scrambled down Gordon's tree and headed towards Paulo's.

"Oh, no you don't!" shouted Paulo, hurling his own underwear at my tree. I realized at that moment that I had won the game. I alone now held the key to survival – *the last pair of underwear!* But whose tree should I throw them at? And then it dawned on me! Rip them in half, throw a piece at both trees, and then climb down my tree and run like mad!

"I'll miss you guys!" I said, tossing my torn underwear in two different directions at once. And then it happened. A truck came whipping down the dirt road, dust and pebbles flying.

"We're saved!" yelled Gordon, but to our horror, the truck didn't stop. It sped right past us!

"We're doomed!" said Paulo. Then, through the dust, we could see brake lights! The truck skidded to a stop and reversed! It was coming to our rescue, and just in the nick of time. The bear was halfway up Gordon's tree!

With its horn blaring, the truck backed up to the clearing where we were perched, naked, in our trees. The noise frightened the bear, who quickly scampered down the tree and disappeared into the woods. Gordon, Paulo and I wasted no time in climbing down our trees. When we were about halfway down, the driver rolled down the window and stuck his head out. Only it wasn't *his* head, it was *her* head. The driver was none other than Mrs. Hoagsbrith!

We froze mid-descent. Was it better to be eaten by a bear, or to be seen naked by our teacher. For a split-second we clung to our trees, trying to decide which fate was worse. Then, out of nowhere, the bear reappeared and headed straight towards us again!

"Hurry up!" yelled our teacher. "Forget about your clothes! Just run for the truck!!" The bear began to run. Gordon, Paulo and I sprinted for the truck and dove into the back seat, slamming the door just as the bear reached the clearing and began tearing up our clothes!

Mrs. Hoagsbrith reached for her cell phone as she pulled out of the clearing. "Mrs. Smith? This is Mrs. Hoagsbrith. I found your son and his friends outside of town, sitting naked in three trees, trying not to be eaten by a bear... Pardon?... Yes, I know. Boys will be boys. Can you come to my house and bring three sets of clothes with you?...Thanks. Bye!"

As the truck pulled into our teacher's driveway a few minutes later, Mrs. H. said, "Well boys, I can *usually* keep a secret, but if you expect me to keep this story to myself and not tell the rest of the kids in class about finding you on the side of the road like this, I expect perfect attendance, perfect behaviour, and all your homework completed for the rest of the school year! Deal?"

Chapter 2

A Teachable Moment

Last Saturday, our principal and his wife were walking downtown. While waiting to cross the street, Mr. Evans noticed an empty coffee cup lying on the ground. He bent over, picked it up and tossed it into a nearby garbage can. Instantly, four newsmen with cameras jumped out of their cars and began snapping his picture. Then, a limousine pulled up alongside the curb and our mayor got out and approached the startled principal.

Pumping Mr. Evans' hand up and down, the mayor said, "Congratulations, Mr. Evans! You are the first winner of this town's Good Citizen Prize!" He pinned a large blue ribbon on the principal's chest, shook his hand vigorously once again and smiled for the cameras, explaining, "I personally put that coffee cup on the ground to see if anyone would stop and pick it up. Many people walked right by it, but you stopped and picked it up and threw it in the trash can. I am proud to have you as a citizen of my town!" Then, the mayor got back into his limo and drove off. The cameramen left as well, leaving Mr. Evans and his wife on the sidewalk, alone and speechless.

"Well," said our principal at last, puffing out his chest proudly. "What do you think of that? Imagine me, winning our town's Good Citizen award. Not every wife is lucky enough to be married to a blue ribbon winner!"

"Lucky me," said Mrs. Evans, yawning. "Why don't you go to your office and write a speech about winning the blue ribbon for the kids at school, and I'll celebrate by going shopping and spending some money on myself."

"Great idea!" exclaimed our principal, his eyes glossing over. "Yes, the kids will want to hear all about my Good Citizen ribbon. I can use this as an opportunity to teach them many things. There's nothing kids like better than being preached to by an adult. It's why they love coming to school!"

* * * * *

When we arrived at school on Monday morning, Mr. Evans was wearing his blue ribbon as he greeted everyone out on the playground. He explained how he had been given the ribbon by the mayor because he was the best citizen in town. The little kids applauded while the older kids just rolled their eyes. Then Mr. Evans dashed inside to prepare his special morning announcement.

After rushing through the regular announcements, the principal cleared his throat and launched into the longest announcement in the history of Danglemore Public School. "Many of you may have heard a rumour that I am now famous," he began. "And I'd just like to set the record straight. The rumour is absolutely --- true! I, your principal and leader of this school, am now the most famous and important citizen of this town. Many of you students look up to Mrs. Hoagsbrith, who has been teaching longer than any other teacher in the school board. But has she ever won a blue ribbon for good citizenship? No! And many of you students look up to Gordon Smith, who will probably be here longer than any other student in the history of this school. But has he ever won a blue ribbon for good citizenship? Again, no!"

I watched as Gordon and Mrs. Hoagsbrith locked eyes and a silent message seemed to pass between them.

The announcement went on for another ten minutes, and by the end of it, half the kids were asleep. At recess, Mr. Evans, who was usually nowhere to be seen, paraded around the playground wearing his blue ribbon and telling teachers exactly what they were doing wrong while on yard duty. It was only worse at lunch recess, when Mr. Evans told the yard duty supervisors, the teachers and the students how they, too, could improve themselves and become model citizens of our town. "You can all learn from me," he said. "Not just because I am the principal of this school and therefore better and smarter than the rest of you, but because I have the Blue Ribbon for Good Citizenship!"

It went on like that all day. Mr. Evans interrupted classes with announcements on how we could become model citizens at school, how we could become good role models for other students at other schools, and ways in which the teachers could become role models if only they would follow his own example and be more like him.

Then, just before last recess, I saw Mrs. Hoagsbrith pull Gordon aside and whisper something in his ear. The two of them high-fived each other.

Just like the two recesses before, Mr. Evans was again strutting around the school yard, bothering teachers and kids with more of his unwanted advice. Just as he was about to address a pack of little kids playing in the sand, Gordon approached him and said, "Excuse me, Mr. Evans." He held up a crisp $20 bill. "I will give you $20 if you pick up that old piece of chewing gum over there and throw it in the garbage." Everyone looked at the piece of gum on the tarmac. It had a few hairs and some small stones stuck to it. For a moment, the principal looked angry, but then he smiled.

"Gather 'round, everyone!" he shouted. "This is a great teachable moment! Gordon Smith thinks that I, a great award-winning principal, am too important to pick up a dirty old piece of gum lying on the ground for the price of $20. I accept his challenge. There are a great many things that can be learned here, so listen and watch!" Mr. Evans bent down and picked up the gooey mess of gum, hair and stones with his bare hand and held it up for all to see. With his other hand, he plucked the $20 out of Gordon's fist. "This money shall be donated to the Teacher's Overseas Charity," he said, handing it to the closest teacher. Everyone gasped. Mr. Evans was not known for his generosity. In fact, he was well-known around school for just the opposite. He was what we once overheard the teachers calling him – stingy and tight-fisted.

"Now," Mr. Evans gloated. "Let's see what we have learned here. Number one: the pavement is now clean and gum-free. Number two: an overseas charity is now $20 richer. And number three: Gordon has foolishly lost his hard-earned money." In a quieter tone, he added, "By the way, Gordon, where did you get that money anyway? Was it a birthday gift? Christmas money? Taken from your savings?" And then it happened.

"Nope," said Gordon gleefully. "Mrs. H. told me she owed you $20 for the staff coffee fund and asked me to give it to you at recess. Raising his voice, Gordon said, "Now, let's review what we have learned. Number one:

our school pavement is now clean and gum-free. Number two: an overseas charity is $20 richer. And number three: Mr. Evans is out $20! By the way, Mr. Evans," gloated Gordon. "Where will you get the money to pay for Mrs. H's coffee from? Your birthday money? Your Christmas money or your savings?"

As we watched Mr. Evans chase Gordon around the school yard, his blue ribbon fell off and was blown away by the breeze.

Chapter 3

The Big Flush

It was the end of January, and for the first time anyone could remember, our town had no snow at all. All the kids at school were grumbling about not being able to go snowboarding or have snowball fights, but for Gordon, the complete lack of snow was cause for greater concern.

"We usually have 3 or 4 snow days in January alone, and this year, we've had none," he complained. "All this school is stressing me out. Plus, I could really use a few days away from Mrs. H. She's really getting on my nerves."

"Yup," agreed Paulo. "Spring is right around the corner, and it looks like we won't have a single snow day this year."

In the staff room at Danglemore Public School, a similar conversation was taking place.

"I don't remember a year without snow," sighed Mrs. Hoagsbrith. "And more importantly, a few good snow days. I'd do anything for a few days without students, just to get caught up. Plus, I could really use some time away from Gordon. He's really stressing me out." All the teachers nodded in agreement and looked longingly out the window, hoping to see some sign of snow in the sky.

"Look on the bright side," said Mr. Evans. "At least we don't have to worry about those darn snow hills!"

Later that afternoon, the sun came out and the temperature rose even higher. At recess, kids took off their heavy winter coats. Hats and mitts littered the playground.

"I can't take it anymore," said Gordon. "Boys, desperate times call for desperate measures. If Mother Nature won't snow on her own, we'll let Mother Science do it for her."

"How can science make it snow?" I asked.

"Easy," replied Gordon with a gleam in his eye. "I read in a science magazine, or was it a cartoon I saw... I can't remember, but whatever. It said that if you flush 10 ice cubes down the toilet before going to bed, it will snow the next day! So if I can get every kid in school to flush 10 ice cubes down the toilet tonight, we'll have a huge blizzard by tomorrow!!"

"I don't believe it," said Paulo.

"It's true!" insisted Gordon. "They said that flushing ice cubes down the toilet caused it to snow 3 out of 2 times!"

"Three out of two times?" I gasped. I liked those odds. "Count me in!"

Gordon, Paulo and I spent the rest of recess running around telling everyone about our plan. It was called *Operation Big Flush* and it was top secret. No parents and no teachers were allowed to hear of our plan, and that night, an entire town of kids snuck ten ice cubes out of their freezers and flushed them down the toilet before going to bed. Naturally, many kids, including Gordon, figured that if ten ice cubes did the trick, then 20 or even 30 ice cubes would work even better! I went to bed that night with a smile on my face, while visions of snowflakes danced in my head.

When I awoke the next morning, I sprang from my
bed, flew to the window and threw up the sash. And then
it happened. What I saw caused my jaw to drop in
disbelief: clear blue skies and not a single snowflake in
sight. The grass had never looked greener and I swore I
heard robins chirping. I would never trust science again.

Gordon looked as miserable as I did as we slowly
made our way to school that morning, dragging our feet.
We were met at the gates of the playground by an angry
mob of students demanding to know what had gone
wrong. *Why was there no snow? Where was the blizzard
we had promised?* ***When were we going to get our snow
day??*** Luckily the bell rang just then and we made our
getaway. Once safely in our seats, we were met by the
angry glares of our classmates. Just when I was thinking
that this was going to be a very long, difficult day, Mr.
Evans made an announcement.

"May I have your attention, please," he said, sounding
very light-hearted and cheerful. "I regret to inform you
that *all* of the public buildings in town are experiencing
difficulties with their plumbing, including Danglemore
Public School. None of the toilets at school are flushing

properly, and only ice water is coming out of the fountains. Apparently, huge chunks of ice are clogging up the entire town's sewage system, and unfortunately, we will have to close the school until the problem is sorted out."

Cries of joy and whoops could be heard all over the school, and then the students joined in the teachers' celebration. Grabbing our backpacks, we stampeded out the doors of the school and headed home to enjoy our first ever Ice Day!

Chapter 4

Brain Food

It was Wednesday, lunch time. Gordon, Paulo and I had been sent to the principal's office for fighting. *Fighting?* I thought, as the teachers pulled us apart. *Who's fighting?* Gordon had simply grabbed my last candy and popped it into his mouth, and I had simply punched him in the stomach to try and make him cough it out. When that didn't work, I tackled him. Not wanting to be accused of taking sides, Paulo had jumped on top of the two of us, and then all three of us had rolled around on the ground, kicking and coughing in the dust and dirt.

As we waited outside the principal's office, a man in a white lab coat walked up to us and said, "I am Doctor Hawkins. I'd like to see your principal."

I looked at his name badge and sure enough, it said, Dr. Hawkins, PhB.

"What do you want with our principal?" asked Gordon.

"I want to show him how he can turn every C student into an A student," said Dr. Hawkins, confidently.

Our principal must have overheard this because he rushed out of his office. "Dr. Hawkins! "What brings such a great man as yourself to our humble school?" Mr. Evans gushed.

"Well, I understand that your school has some of the lowest test scores in the district. Who are we kidding? In the entire country!"

"Yes," agreed our principal, frowning. "Our students spend too much of their energy fighting and wrestling instead of studying and reading." He threw a glance in our direction.

"Well, I am a great man of science, and I can solve all of your problems for you," promised Dr. Hawkins. "If you do as I say, your students will get straight A's in school and have no energy, I mean, time, for fighting and wrestling."

"Our principal gasped and fell onto his knees.

"Please!" he begged. "I'll do anything!"

"You see, the trouble is with these kids' brains," explained Dr. Hawkins. "Brains are directly related to one's diet. The animal with the biggest brain is the blue whale. And do you know what blue whales eat?"

"No," said our principal. Gordon, Paulo and I didn't have a clue either, but Dr. Hawkins continued without waiting for an answer. "They eat *krill*. That's right! The animals with the biggest brains eat krill and *only krill*. Three meals a day! Krill for breakfast, lunch and dinner, and if your students eat krill for breakfast, lunch and dinner, they will increase the size of their brains and go from having the lowest test scores in the country to the highest test scores in the country."

Now, our principal was no dummy. He was highly educated himself and he recognized a great scientist when he met one. "How can I get my hands on some krill?" he begged.

"Funny you should ask," said Dr. Hawkins. "I just happen to have a full van of delicious, nutritious, ready-to-eat krill right outside. It will cost you only $10,000 for enough krill to feed your students breakfast, lunch and dinner for one full day. I understand you're having a Board-wide test the day after tomorrow?"

"We most certainly are!" said Mr. Evans. "And with your wonderful krill, my school could go from being the lowest in the country to the highest! I might even be promoted from principal to Superintendent! No more students, no more teachers, just endless lunch meetings where we invent new policies and *pilot projects with impossible-to-remember acronyms!!*" Our principal's eyes glazed over and he stared into space for a full minute before coming back to reality. "Boys!" he snapped, noticing Gordon, Paulo and me still sitting on the bench. "Help Dr. Hawkins bring his krill in here while I write a school cheque for $10,000."

As we carried in the heavy boxes, I noticed a label on the side of each one that said NOT FOR HUMAN CONSUMPTION.

"What does that mean?" I asked Dr. Hawkins.

"Oh, uh, um, that means that it's not meant for adults. We're already smart enough. But I'm sure it's fine for kids."

Coming out of his office, cheque in hand, Mr. Evans said, "And will you be staying in town for a few days to see how well this marvelous product works on our students, Doctor?"

"Me? Oh, good heavens, no. I've got some important science business to conduct at the nearest bank and then I'll be moving on." He plucked the cheque for $10,000 out of the principal's hand, spun on his heel and was gone in a flash.

"There goes a great man," sighed Mr. Evans, looking dreamily at the boxes of krill lying on the floor. "Just think, finally, my students – as smart as whales!"

*   *   *   *   *

Before school ended that day, Mr. Evans announced that tomorrow, every student would be given all their meals at school, including breakfast, lunch and dinner. We were not even allowed to bring any candy, chips, pop or other junk food to school. Tomorrow, we would be eating nothing but krill, the ultimate brain food!

When we arrived at school the following morning, every student was handed a warm bowl of krill and a spoon the minute they stepped onto the playground. I overheard a couple of little kids.

"What's this stuff?"

"I don't know. It's supposed to be good for you."

"I'm not gonna eat it."

"Well, I'm not gonna eat it, either."

"I know! Let's get Gordon! He'll eat anything!" And while that was usually true, even Gordon was having a hard time getting the warm, soggy krill down the hatch. Krill was without a doubt the worst-tasting food in the entire world. It was salty and fishy-tasting. Blue whales might have the biggest brains, but they must also have the smallest sense of taste and smell. If it weren't for the teachers wandering around the playground making sure that we ate every single bit of krill in our bowls, no one would have touched the stuff. We had no other choice. No one was allowed to go home that day until they had eaten their three bowls of krill.

At noon, Mr. Evans came on the announcements just as we were sitting down to our second bowl of krill. He said that while it might taste horrible, we would be happy we had eaten it today because tomorrow, when we took the Board-wide test, we would breeze through it and our grades would be higher than ever.

Just before the end of the day, we were given our third and final bowl of krill, and Mr. Evans gave one final announcement. "I'm holding the bell, and no one is allowed to leave until their bowl is empty. And I want all of you to get a good night's sleep. Tomorrow is the Board-wide test, and Danglemore Public School is going to do us all proud for once."

I wasn't feeling too well, and I wanted nothing more than to go home and lie down. Looking around the room, I could see that several others, including Gordon and Paulo, actually looked a little green. We quickly finished our krill and staggered home.

And then it happened. It hit me at 8 o'clock that night. I was sweating and I had a high fever. My mom phoned some other parents, and it turned out that every kid in school was sick. The emergency room was overflowing, and parents were told that their kids had krill poisoning. It wasn't serious, they said. Just go home, put the kids to bed for a day or two, and they would be back to normal in no time. We were all advised to stay home from school the next day.

* * * * *

The following Monday, when we were all back at school, our principal announced that since no one had shown up to write the Board-wide test, our school was given a big fat zero! Never in the history of testing had a school scored a perfect zero.

"I was so sick from that krill," I told Gordon and Paulo at recess. "When I woke up the next morning, I felt like I had swallowed half an ocean. I ran to the bathroom, but nothing came out for *two hours* even though I was desperate to go!"

"That's nothing," said Paulo. "I was so sick and cramped up, I woke up at 6 am but I couldn't go to the bathroom for *three* hours no matter how hard I strained!"

Gordon shook his head and said, "You guys got nothing on me. I was so sick, I had *no* trouble going to the bathroom at 7 o'clock the next morning, no straining whatsoever. Number 1 *and 2!*"

"How does that make you sicker than us?" I demanded.

28

"Because I didn't wake up until 8 o'clock!" said Gordon.

Chapter 5

The Principal's Underwear

It was Thursday afternoon, and any minute, the bell would ring to end the day. Mrs. Hoagsbrith stood in front of the class and said, "Now don't forget, tomorrow is a PD Day so you lucky kids get to stay home while the teachers have to go to an education conference."

Gordon raised his hand and asked, "What do you do at an education conference?"

"We listen to talks by education experts on how to become better teachers. Tomorrow's topic is all about student discipline," our teacher explained.

"What's an education expert?" asked Gordon.

"Oh," explained Mrs. H. "An education expert is someone that doesn't teach or have any contact with children. For those reasons, they are greatly admired and respected by teachers because if they can have a career in education without actually having to work with children, then they must be *much* smarter than the rest of us."

Paulo leaned over and whispered to me, "What does that mean?"

"Don't ask me," I replied. "I tuned out after she said, *'stay home tomorrow.'*"

The bell rang and everyone headed home for a wonderful three day weekend.

* * * * *

When we arrived at school the following Monday, we were surprised to see smiles on the faces of the yard duty teachers. There was a strange spring in their step, and they smiled at each other and exchanged knowing glances as if they shared some secret. *That was odd,* I thought, *especially on a Monday morning.* Normally, on a Monday morning, the teachers just walked slowly around the playground with cups of coffee in their hands, staring off into space, already counting the days until Friday.

"Uh-oh," said Gordon. "I don't like this one bit. Something happened at that PD Day. *They're up to something.*"

When the bell rang, we were told to go straight to the gym for a special announcement. Once the entire school was assembled, Mr. Evans stood up on the stage and began.

"Last Friday, the teachers and I attended a wonderful PD session in which we were told that we had been handling school discipline all wrong. The experts taught how we could have complete control over our students while making life easier for us. In the past, whenever anyone misbehaved, they were sent to the office or made to stay in for recess. In some extreme cases, we called home and spoke to their parents, and on rare occasions (I swear he glanced at Gordon when he said this) suspensions were given out for particularly bad behaviour. These techniques all worked in the past, when children had respect for their elders and feared their teachers and their parents, but nowadays, kids don't fear a phone call home or even a suspension. So we were taught to find out what it is that you kids fear the most, and that will become the new punishment. Your teachers and I will therefore spend the next few days figuring out what it is that you fear the most. And finally, the kids in this school will all behave beautifully." There was a scattering of applause around the gym as the teachers all showed their enthusiasm for this new plan. "The assembly is over. You may return to your classrooms."

Naturally, the topic at morning recess was all about what the new punishment would be. The playground buzzed with kids talking about what they feared the most and how they hoped the teachers would never find out what that was. Gordon, Paulo and I were sitting on the pavement, leaning up against the school wall, well away from the yard duty teachers who might overhear our conversation.

I said, "I'll bet the new punishment will be that we have to wash all the teachers' cars."

Paulo said, "No. I'll bet the punishment will be that we have to cut all the teachers' toenails!"

"I'll bet the new punishment will be that we have to wash the principal's underwear by hand!" said Gordon.

"That's just sick, Gordon!" I said.

The bell rang to end recess and we quietly filed back into the building. Meanwhile, unbeknownst to us, we had been sitting directly under the window to the principal's office, and Mr. Evans had heard every word. He grinned now, rubbing his hands together gleefully. "That's perfect!" he chuckled.

The rest of the day passed with no mention from Mr. Evans or our teachers about what the new punishment would be, but when we arrived the next morning, there were posters taped all over the building. They were on every door and window and covering most of the walls in the hallways. The pictures on the posters were all the same. They showed a crying kid holding a pail of soapy water in one hand, and in the other hand, a pair of very large underwear. The message below read, *This Could Happen to You!* Others said, *Behave, or Else You Will Be the Student in this Picture!*

In one second flat, every kid in the school was on their best behaviour. For the rest of the day, not one kid did anything wrong. Little kids remembered to raise their hands. No one cried if they couldn't be the caboose in line. No one picked their nose. In the older grades, not one piece of litter fell on the floor. No one ran in the halls. No one budded, shoved or pushed while in line. No one rolled their eyes at their teacher or called anyone an inappropriate name. In short, the fear of washing the principal's underwear instantly turned us into perfect students.

On Tuesday morning, the principal came on the announcements and said, "Yesterday, not one student was sent to my office. I made absolutely no phone calls home. The teachers reported that their students all behaved perfectly. All homework was completed, and all assignments were turned in on time. It was the best day I've ever had as principal of Danglemore Public School. Keep up the good work! Oh, and a word of warning..." Here his voice took on a Grinch-like sneer. "It is Tuesday, I am now wearing *two-day-old underwear.* So don't slip up!!" Four hundred students all shivered in unison.

On Wednesday, Mr. Evans made a similar announcement, stating that our school had been so quiet and so well-behaved, that he actually saw three teachers skipping with joy at the end of the day. We were warned once again about the punishment for misbehaving – only now the underwear was *three days old*. If that didn't strike fear into every student's heart, nothing would.

When the morning announcements were made on Thursday, we expected another pat on the back for how well we were behaving, and another warning about the principal's underwear, but that isn't what happened. Instead, Mr. Evans told us how proud he was of all of us, and, as a special treat, he had convinced the local theatre to lift its life-time ban on Danglemore Public School students from ever stepping foot in the theatre again. Because we were now so well-behaved, they agreed to let us have one more chance at watching a play, and on Friday morning, we were all being bused to the theatre. Mr. Evans was even going to buy everyone popcorn as a reward for our outstanding behaviour. Normally, this would have been followed by loud cheering, whistling, and foot-stomping, but the threat of the principal's dirty underwear still hung heavy in the air. Instead, we politely clapped and kept our mouths firmly shut.

The next morning, everyone was on time to catch the buses for the theatre. Our clothes were clean, our faces washed, and our teeth brushed. We waited in perfectly straight lines to board the buses. We rode to the theatre in well-behaved silence. We left the buses in the same orderly silence, and we entered the theatre in beautifully straight lines that would have made an army drill sergeant proud. We held the doors for our teachers. We sat down in our rows and kept our eyes to the front of the theatre and our mouths shut.

Just before the curtain rose to start the play, Mr. Evans stood on the stage and gave us one final warning. "If anyone, and I mean *anyone*, from my school disrupts this play in any way, we will return to school and everyone will watch that person wash "The Day Five Underwear." He climbed down off the stage.

The curtain rose and we all enjoyed the first act of the play. Our class had the best seats in the house – front row! Much of the theatre was taken up by our school, but there were also members of the public and some seniors from the local nursing home who had also arrived by bus to watch the play. Not taking any chances, Mrs.

Hoagsbrith had separated Gordon, Paulo and me by placing a senior citizen in between each of us, and she sat on the other side of Gordon so he was sandwiched between our teacher and an old man that looked to be about one hundred years old. When the curtain fell to end the first act, our entire school politely applauded and remained in our seats until our teachers told us what to do. We were allowed to go to the washroom or get a drink, and when we returned, ushers handed out the bags of popcorn that Mr. Evans had purchased for us. Every single student remembered to thank the usher when they were handed a bag of popcorn, and we all sat munching quietly as we waited for the curtain to rise for the second act. Even Mrs. Hoagsbrith was enjoying a bag of popcorn, and for once, I thought she actually looked happy and relaxed. The lights dimmed, and the curtain rose.

The moment the play resumed, the old man next to Gordon suddenly twitched. His head snapped sideways and clunked heavily onto Gordon's shoulder. Not wanting to get into trouble and be forced to wash out the principal's underwear by hand, Gordon stared straight

ahead and concentrated on the play, not moving a muscle.
He barely dared to breathe. Suddenly, the old man bolted
straight upright in his seat. Gordon didn't even turn to
look at him. He just kept his eyes on the actors onstage.
A moment later, the man emitted a violent, rattling cough.
His head rolled to one side, and his false teeth flew out of
his mouth, shot across Gordon's lap, landing in Mrs.
Hoagsbrith's popcorn bag! Our teacher was so relaxed
and caught up in the play, she failed to notice anything
that was going on around her. The old man gave a final
soft moan, fell against Gordon, and remained there,
unmoving. Still, Gordon did nothing. He didn't make a
sound. He didn't budge from his seat. The fear of having
a dead man leaning against him in a darkened theatre was
nothing compared to his fear of having to wash out the
principal's 5-day-old underwear! The play continued on.
The audience laughed and chuckled, and kids continued to
quietly chew their popcorn. I noticed that Mrs.
Hoagsbrith really seemed to be enjoying the play. Not
having to worry about what her class was up to for once,
she was able to give it her undivided attention. I watched
as she stared at the stage and absent-mindedly reached

into her popcorn bag. Grabbing a big handful of popcorn, she shoveled it into her mouth. And then it happened. Mrs. H. bit down on something hard. Reaching into her mouth she pulled out the old man's teeth. Then she noticed the man leaning up against Gordon with his mouth open *and empty!* She quickly put two and two together. Letting out an ear-piercing scream, our teacher leapt up onto the stage in a move that would have impressed an Olympic gymnast. She began dancing around wildly and spitting on the stage to get the taste of the old man's teeth out of her mouth, and she finished by wiping her face on the nearest actress's dress. All the actors screamed and ran to get away from the crazy woman attacking them onstage. Alarmed at what was happening, many people in the audience jumped up and stampeded for the exits, trampling each other and knocking over all the tables and chairs in the lobby. Only the students from Danglemore Public School remained in their seats, perfectly well-behaved. The teachers quickly ushered us back onto the buses as Mr. Evans ran after Mrs. Hoagsbrith. The theatre manager yelled and shook his fist at our buses as they pulled away from the theatre. It was the first time I'd ever seen a bus do a burn-out.

As our buses pulled into the parking lot of the school fifteen minutes later, we looked out the windows. An incredible sight met our eyes. Marching out to the middle of the playground was Mrs. H., a bucket of soapy water in one hand, and the principal's underwear on the end of a long stick in the other.

Chapter 6

Up, Up and Away

Every spring, our school holds a big fundraiser to raise money for things like new computers, class trips and playground equipment. It's an annual event that we used to look forward to. The parents and teachers work for weeks putting together a carnival in the school yard, and for one night, kids and their families can come and play games, try to dunk their favourite teacher in the dunk tank, or have their fortune told. When we were little, we thought the school carnival was better than the town fair, but now that we were older, we thought it was a little lame. Year after year, the same old games were played, the same prizes were handed out, and we were beginning to suspect that the "fortune teller" really had no clue as to what our futures held. Last year, she told Gordon that he would become a better student, complete all of his homework, and finish at the top of his class. Anyone from grade 1 up could have told her that *that* wasn't going to happen. No one needed a crystal ball to see that! So this year, when Mrs. Hoagsbrith told us that there was going to be a new attraction at the carnival, we really weren't all that excited.

"What is it?" sighed Gordon. "Pin the tail on the donkey? A ring toss game?"

"No," said our teacher. "I think even you'll be surprised, Gordon." We waited in anticipation. "It's a brand-new idea. This year, the school is renting a hot air balloon! It will be tethered in the school yard and for $5.00, kids can go up in the balloon and get an amazing view of our town."

There were murmurs of *ooh* and *aah* around the room, and even Gordon was impressed. Everyone wanted to ride in the hot air balloon.

* * * * *

The night of the carnival finally arrived. The brightly striped balloon could be seen from all over town and as far away as Paulo's farm. Our parents had given us all money to spend at the carnival, and we wanted to be the first ones to go up in the balloon. But when we arrived at the carnival, there was already a huge line of people waiting for a balloon ride.

"I guess we should have gotten here earlier," said Paulo.

"I don't want to stand in that line all night," said Gordon. "Why don't we see what else there is to do and wait for the line to go down?"

So we wandered around the carnival for the next hour and a half. We tried a few of the games, won a few prizes, and ate a lot of food. Gordon even decided to have his fortune told again. Entering the fortune teller's tent, Gordon sat down at a small round table across from a woman in a long flowing gown. Bracelets lined her arms, and earrings hung to her shoulders. She jangled and jingled with every move she made. She looked much more authentic than last year's fortune teller. Paulo and I waited quietly at the edge of the tent to hear what she had to say.

"Give me your hand," she told Gordon in a low, husky voice tinged with an exotic accent. Gordon held out his right hand. She took it in one of her hands and traced a line down Gordon's palm with her index finger.

"Ahh," murmured the fortune teller. "You have a very interesting hand, young man. I can see much in your future. You will live a long life, acquire great riches, and have many sons much like yourself. But I see trouble ahead for you as well. I see bars and locked doors. But fear not. You will have your trusty companions by your side."

Paulo and I nervously glanced at each other. *Trouble? Bars and locked doors? I always suspected Gordon would end up in jail, and now he was going to drag me and Paulo along with him!!*

"What else do you see?" I asked quickly.

"Nothing. That is all," said the fortune teller. "Five dollars, please."

Gordon handed over his money and we left the tent.

When we were down to our last $5.00, we got in line for the hot air balloon. By this time, most of the kids had been up in the balloon, and we didn't have to wait long. Since the balloon was tethered to the ground, the man running the balloon booth didn't have to actually go up in the balloon. He could operate it from the ground.

As we approached the front of the line, Gordon said quietly, "Look at that guy. He looks bored, and see how he keeps sipping from that water bottle?"

"He's been doing that all night," said Paulo. "Every time I looked over to see if the line had gone down, the guy was taking a drink from his bottle."

Finally our turn to go up in the hot air balloon arrived.

"Step right up, boys, *hic!* Don't be shy! *Hic!*" *He's got a bad case of hiccups*, I thought, but I quickly forgot about the man as I eagerly hopped into the basket. Once Gordon, Paulo and I were safely in the basket and the little door was shut, the man began letting out the rope that held the hot air balloon in place, and we slowly rose up over the playground.

"Cool," said Paulo. "This is awesome!"

"I can see your house, Gordon!" I exclaimed excitedly.

"This is pretty neat," admitted Gordon, scanning the horizon. "I can see the mall and the train tracks, and there's the high school and that new subdivision over there."

"Uh, guys," I said nervously, looking directly down at the playground again. "Where's the guy who was operating the balloon? I don't see him anywhere!"

"Oh, he probably just went to the bathroom after drinking all that water," said Gordon. "Maybe we'll get a longer turn!"

A few minutes passed and the man didn't return. By now we were growing a little bored with the view.

"Did you guys notice that the wind seems to have come up?" asked Paulo.

"Oh, yeah," I said. "We're starting to swing around a bit. I can see your farm over those trees, Paulo."

We craned our necks to enjoy the new view. The basket was really moving around by this point, and still there was no sign of the man operating the balloon. Dusk was setting in.

"We sure are getting our money's worth," said Gordon.

"I shouldn't have eaten so much," I groaned. "I think I'm gonna throw up."

I leaned over the side of the balloon, and that's when I noticed it! One of the ropes that held the balloon in place had snapped! That's why we were moving around so much!

"Guys!" I shouted. "One of the ropes is loose, and I don't see the guy anywhere!"

The wind began blowing harder, and people on the playground began to notice that the balloon was really swaying around. Suddenly, there was a loud CRACK! Another rope had snapped and the basket rocked precariously. We started shouting but the wind caught our voices and carried them away. By now, people were pointing and running towards the hot air balloon booth. There was still no sign of the man in charge of the balloon. Another huge gust of wind shook the basket, and the third rope snapped, and then the fourth! We were no longer tethered to the ground!!

"Oh, my gosh!" I shouted

"Help!" yelled Paulo.

"This is so cool!" exclaimed Gordon. "Now we'll get a *real* ride in this thing!"

The balloon drifted away from the school yard and over the town. I was too scared to notice the view, but Gordon kept on pointing things out. "Look! There's the town pool! And there's McDonald's!"

"Who cares, Gordon?" I shouted. "Does anyone know how to land this thing?"

"Land it?" said Gordon. "We just got it going!"

"I think all we have to do," said Paulo, "is let some of the hot air out through that top vent."

"But how do we open the vent?" I asked anxiously.

"I don't know," admitted Paulo. "There are all these ropes…" his voice drifted away.

"There's the airport," said Gordon cheerfully. "You guys are really missing a great view."

"Let's try pulling on a rope," I suggested. "Things can't get any worse, right?"

"Okay," agreed Paulo nervously. "Here goes!" He grabbed a rope and gave a tug. Nothing happened. He tugged harder and the balloon started to rise.

"Wrong rope!!" I yelled.

"There's the lake," said Gordon calmly.

"Try another rope, Paulo!" I shouted. He grabbed a rope at random and tugged. Instantly we felt a drop in height! The vent at the top of the balloon had opened up and we were heading down!

"Try to land in that farmer's field," I said, pointing.

"If you have any idea how to steer this thing, be my guest!" said Paulo. *OK. So steering wasn't going to happen.*

The balloon continued to drift towards the outskirts of town as it slowly descended. Gordon continued pointing out all the sights. "There's the drive-in!" he called. "Hey, we can watch the movie from here!"

"Get ready to touch down soon!" I yelled as the balloon got lower and lower. "About another minute or so should do it."

"Cool!" shouted Gordon excitedly. "I can see the jail from here!"

The jail! Paulo and I stared at each other.

"Not there!" I shouted.

"Beggars can't be choosers!" Paulo shouted back.

We watched in horror as the balloon slowly drifted over a large building enclosed in a high fence topped with razor wire. Suddenly the basket was filled with a blinding white flash as search lights zeroed in on us. A voice boomed out over a loud speaker.

"People in the balloon! This is a restricted area. Do not land your craft here. Repeat. DO NOT LAND HERE!"

And then it happened. *Bump!* The balloon hit the ground and rose a few feet. *Bump!* It hit the ground again and came to a rest in a large courtyard. Instantly we were surrounded by men in uniforms. Orange uniforms! These weren't guards! They were prisoners! The courtyard was filled with prisoners!

"Out of the basket!" a rough voice ordered. Large hands grabbed us and threw us to the ground. Guards raced toward the balloon, but not before several inmates jumped into the basket, pulled at the ropes, and began to rise up over the courtyard!

"STOP THAT BALLOON!" ordered the guards, but it was too late. The balloon sailed gracefully over the heads of the prisoners, the guards, and Gordon, Paulo and me as we stood helplessly on the ground, watching it drift away.

* * * * *

By the next day, Gordon, Paulo and I were famous, not for surviving a run-away balloon ride, but for being accomplices in the largest prison break in our town's history. We were forced to spend several hours behind bars while we tried to explain what had really happened. Not even the principal or our parents could convince the prison guards that we really had nothing to do with the break-out. We were fingerprinted and had our mug shots taken. It was the worst night of my life!

At the crack of dawn the next morning, two guards came and shouted at us to wake up. Apparently, the prisoners who had escaped in the hot air balloon were captured when they ran out of gas and the balloon landed in a football field! The prisoners told the police that Gordon, Paulo and I had nothing to do with their break-out, and we were being released at last!

"Well, look on the bright side," said Gordon when we finally regained our freedom and were heading home. "At least now we won't have to spend the rest of our lives wondering if we really *would* end up behind bars like that fortune teller predicted! That's already happened!!"

Chapter 7

Things Can Always Get Worse

It was the end of May, and Gordon, Paulo and I were about to celebrate the last three-day weekend of the school year by going camping. We had no homework, the weather forecast called for clear, sunny skies all weekend, and our parents had agreed to drive us out to the woods after school and drop us off for the entire weekend. It was a little past six pm when Gordon's mom dropped us off on a deserted dirt road next to the woods. Weighed down with our heavy backpacks, we hiked for an hour to our favourite camping spot and dropped our gear.

"Let's set up the tent and then eat," said Paulo. "I'm starving!"

Thirty minutes later, the tent was up, our sleeping bags were rolled out and ready for us when it got dark, and we were opening the food containers Gordon's mother had packed for us.

"Smells delicious!" I said, digging into some spaghetti.

"Tastes delicious, too," agreed Paulo.

"Have some fried chicken," said Gordon, passing a plate around.

"It sure was great of your mom to pack so much food," I said.

"Oh, she was happy to do it," said Gordon. "She said she didn't want us getting hungry and coming home early."

After we had eaten our fill and put away the rest of the food for morning, we decided to get our fishing poles ready. Just as I was tying on a lure, I heard a loud splash on the river behind us.

"Did you guys hear that fish jumping?" I asked. "It sure made a loud splash!"

"Yeah. It must have been huge!" said Gordon excitedly.

"Uh, guys," said Paulo quietly. "It *is* huge, but that was no fish. It's a bear, and he's headed this way!!"

"Oh, no!" whispered Gordon. "He must have smelled our dinner!"

"Okay, everyone," said Paulo. "Remain calm."

"Right!" agreed Gordon and I, dropping our rods and racing to the nearest tree, yelling and shoving each other out of the way in our haste to climb to safety, followed closely by Paulo. We just made it safely up the tree when the bear came crashing boldly into our camp. He shook himself, spraying water all over our tent, and then he proceeded to tear the tent to shreds with his huge claws. He dragged out our sleeping bags and shredded those, as well. Then he spotted us in the tree! He put his massive paws up on the trunk and sniffed the air. Deciding that we were not the spaghetti dinner that he was looking for, the bear turned back to our camp and proceeded to rip through our packs in search of food. We watched as he bit holes in our plastic water bottles and ripped open our snack food and wolfed it down. Unfortunately, this bear was not satisfied with just a snack, and he continued to rip and destroy all of our camping equipment. At last he found what he was looking for and he noisily devoured every last crumb of the food Gordon's mother had packed!

With a full belly, the bear took one last look at us, belched loudly, and disappeared into the growing darkness. We waited for a full ten minutes before speaking.

"Do you think he's gone?" whispered Gordon.

"Yes," I whispered back. "It's probably safe now. Gordon, you climb down and check it out. Paulo and I will stay here and keep you covered."

"Yeah, we got your back," said Paulo encouragingly as Gordon quietly slid down the tree and explored the wrecked camp. Seeing that the coast was clear, Paulo and I bravely climbed down the tree and joined him.

"Well," I said sadly, "we have no food, no clean water, no tent, no sleeping bags and it's going to be completely dark in an hour."

"Hey," said Paulo, "you forgot the good news."

"What's that?" I asked.

"Things can't get any worse!"

If there's one thing I've learned in life, it's that things can *always* get worse!

Suddenly, Gordon went pale. He pointed behind Paulo and me and shouted, *"BEAR!!"* We took off at top speed! We crashed through trees and shrubs until we finally found a path in the woods. We ran until we were completely winded. Finally stopping to catch our breath, we looked around to make sure the bear hadn't followed us. We didn't see anything, but we decided that it still wasn't safe to stay where we were, so we started walking, putting as much distance as possible between us and the bear.

"Look on the bright side. At least there's a full moon so we can see where we're going," said Paulo cheerfully. Gordon and I looked up in time to see a huge bank of clouds roll in and cover the moon, leaving us in total darkness.

"You were saying?" I asked sarcastically.

"I'm exhausted anyway," said Gordon. "Let's stop here and rest until it gets light again in the morning."

"Sounds good to me," I said. We curled up and pulled dry leaves over us for warmth. *Well,* I thought. *At least we can get a good night's sleep.* Just then, the rain started.

We awoke the next morning, sore, cold and wet from our night on the ground. We had no food, our faces, arms and legs were scratched and bloody from running through the woods, and we were totally lost!

"Cheer up! It could be worse," said Paulo.

We spent the entire day trudging through the woods, wandering in circles, and sliding through knee-deep mud. We were starving, filthy, and still totally lost. Worse, it would be dark soon, and I doubted we would survive another cold night in the woods. The rain had stopped, but the mosquitoes were starting to come out in noisy swarms. Just as I was about to open my mouth to say I was ready to give up completely, I heard a sound.

"Did you hear that?" I asked.

"It sounds like voices!" said Gordon.

"Girls' voices," added Paulo, "and they're singing!"

Sure enough, we could hear the faint sound of singing in the distance. We ran in the direction of the sound. It got louder and clearer, and when we finally stopped and parted some bushes, we looked down at the back of a small camp!

"I know this place," said Paulo. "It's Camp Killjoy!"

"I've heard the girls at school talking about this place," I said. "It's a girls' camp, and almost all the girls belong to it." Sure enough, we saw several girls from our class laughing and playing and singing around a big cheery campfire.

"We're saved!" breathed Paulo.

"Oh, no, we're not!" exclaimed Gordon. "I refuse to be rescued by the girls in our class. They will *never* let us live it down. We'll owe them forever and we'll never hear the end of it!"

And then we smelled the delicious aroma of cooking food. One of the counsellors rang a bell and called out, "Come and get it, girls! It's all you can eat!"

Paulo and I looked at Gordon. "Well," he said grudgingly. "Maybe we could just *casually* stroll by their camp. You know, like we were just passing through. They might be kind enough to invite us to dinner. We don't have to let them know that we're lost, starving and freezing to death."

"Sounds good to me!" I yelled as Paulo and I ran full-speed toward the camp. I had my doubts that they would actually feed us. Knowing the girls in our class, I thought it was more likely that they would ignore us and leave us to wander around until we really did starve to death.

"Stay cool and act casual," advised Gordon as we got closer to the camp.

"Right," I said, slowing to a walk. And then I smelled their delicious dinner again! Drooling, I ran forward and threw myself at the feet of the nearest girl, gasping for food and water. I didn't care if they laughed at me or teased me for the rest of my life. I was starving and I wasn't too proud to beg.

"Oh, my goodness!" exclaimed one of the girls. "Look who's here!"

"What are you guys doing here?" cried another girl. Then they noticed our bloodied, filthy faces, arms and legs. We quickly explained about the bear and how we had wandered around in the woods all day after spending the night huddled under a tree. I expected the girls to burst out laughing and make fun of our camping skills, but to my surprise, they instantly took pity on us. Leading us to a table, we were told to sit down while they quickly ran to get us warm plates heaping with food. There was chocolate milk, rolls, and dessert to go with dinner. The girls and their counsellors were so moved by our story and our pitiful condition, they insisted that we spend the night. Three girls even offered to give up their cabin and share with other girls so we could have their cabin.

After we had eaten three helpings of their delicious dinner, they led us to their cabin.

"There are hot showers in there, and lots of clean towels," one of the girls told us. "Feel free to use our cots tonight, and in the morning, we'll have breakfast waiting for you."

We couldn't thank them enough. Not one girl had laughed at us or made fun of us.

After taking nice, hot showers, we fell onto the cots and into a deep sleep, but not before Gordon mumbled, "The girls in our class are the best."

* * * * *

I awoke at first light the next morning. Gordon and Paulo were still softly snoring as I sat up and rubbed my eyes. The camp was quiet and I slipped quietly out of bed to get dressed. I glanced around the cabin for my clothes, which I had carelessly tossed onto a chair last night before my shower. Gordon and Paulo had done the same thing. Now, I noticed, the chair was empty. There was nothing on the floor. Nothing *anywhere!*

"Guys!" I hollered. "Wake up! Our clothes are gone!"

Instantly, Gordon and Paulo were awake. "What do you mean, gone?" asked Paulo. "We put them on that chair last…" his words died away as he spotted the empty chair.

"And notice how quiet the camp is?" I asked. "It's like there's no one here."

"And what about that breakfast the girls promised us?" Paulo asked suspiciously. "I don't smell anything, do you?"

"They tricked us!" exclaimed Gordon. "Those low-down, sneaky girls tricked us!"

"They never meant to be nice," agreed Paulo. "They stole our clothes and left us here in the middle of nowhere! They even took our shoes!"

I ran to the window. Sure enough, the camp looked deserted. Even the vans that the girls had arrived in were gone!

"I'll bet they can't wait to get back to school tomorrow and tell everyone how they left us stranded in the woods naked!" I said.

"We've been outsmarted!" growled Gordon. "Well, two can play at that game!"

"First things first," said Paulo. "We need something to wear." He grabbed a sheet, pulled it off the cot and tied it toga-style around his body.

"Ha! Do you look stupid!" said Gordon, tearing holes in the bottom of a pillowcase to make a pair of shorts for himself.

"It beats the diaper you just put on!" scoffed Paulo.

Torn between wearing a toga and a diaper, I chose the diaper. Mine had unicorns on it. We yanked the rest of the sheets and pillowcases off the other cots and ran outside with them. We threw them into a huge mud puddle and stomped on them, yelling, "Take that, girls!" Next we cut up their blankets to tie around our feet in place of shoes. Then we jumped on their cots until they collapsed on the floor of the cabin. We tied knots in the curtains on the windows and we threw all of their soap as far as we could into the woods. We even dragged their picnic tables into the woods.

"There!" said Gordon, satisfied. "Things at this camp couldn't be worse!" And then we heard a vehicle approaching.

"We're saved!" I shouted happily. "Someone's coming!" And then it happened.

Our smiles quickly faded as we saw several Camp Killjoy vans pull into camp. Out of the vehicles swarmed two dozen girls and their camp counsellors, all smiling and as friendly as the night before.

"We had to go into town to get more groceries for you boys," said one of the counsellors. "You sure ate a lot of our supplies last night."

"And we decided that since we were going into town, we might as well take your clothes and wash them, too," said a girl from our class, holding out a neatly folded pile of clean laundry.

"We even cleaned your muddy shoes," said another girl, smiling. And then she noticed what we were wearing and a frown came to her face. "Are those *my sheets*?"

Then *all* the girls suddenly noticed what we had done to their camp. Looking around at the devastation we had caused, I decided that things *could* get worse. In fact, they were about to get "Guinness Book of World Records" worse!

Chapter 7

The Class Trip

It was the end of June and our class was going on a trip to the Science Centre.

"Cool," said Gordon as we climbed aboard the coach bus that would take us there. "This sure beats an old school bus. There's a washroom, air conditioning and the seats even recline. This trip is going to be awesome!"

Our class had been looking forward to the trip for weeks, ever since our teacher, Mrs. Hoagsbrith, announced that we were going. The Science Centre would be neat, but I was looking forward to the rest stops. We all had money with us and we could spend it on anything we wanted.

The bus pulled out of the school yard at exactly 7:00 am and we were on our way. Gordon reclined his seat back as far as it could go, clasped his hands behind his head, and declared, "Boys, I'm bored already."

"Wanna play a game?" asked Paulo as he reached into the bag he had brought along.

"Nah. That's boring," said Gordon. "But did you guys see what the teachers and parents brought along with them?"

"What?" asked Paulo.

"Coffee. *Extra large* cups of coffee," replied Gordon with a gleam in his eye.

"So?" said Paulo. "What's interesting about coffee?"

"Well," began Gordon. "It's a good thing there's a washroom on this bus, because after drinking all that coffee, they're going to be needing one soon."

"So?" said Paulo again.

"What if the washroom is occupied and they can't get in? That would be kind of fun to watch," answered Gordon mischievously.

Paulo and I grinned at each other. We both felt another

one of Gordon's plots being hatched.

"Let's take turns sitting in the washroom! Paulo, you go first. Don't let anyone in, even if they pound on the door. Say that you have motion sickness or something and tell them to come back later. Don't open the door until I give you the secret knock."

Grinning, Paulo got up from his seat and headed off towards the back of the bus.

Several minutes went by, and then one of the parents rose from his seat, tossed his empty coffee cup in the garbage bag and sauntered down the aisle towards the washroom. He reached out to open the door, and then, realizing it was locked, he turned around and went back to his seat. Gordon smiled at me.

"It's beginning," he whispered.

A minute later another parent got up from her seat and quickly walked towards the washroom. She tried the door handle and when she discovered that it was locked, she knocked on the door. From inside we could hear Paulo's muffled voice say, "I'll be out in a minute." The woman waited outside the door for Paulo to come out. A few more minutes passed and another parent joined the woman in line.

"Hey! This is getting good!" I exclaimed as yet another parent fell into our line.

"What's the holdup," he asked.

"Oh, someone's in there," said the first woman. Gordon rose from his seat to take Paulo's place in the washroom. Hurrying to the back of the bus and squeezing past the line of parents, Gordon held his hand over his mouth as if he were going to be sick. He gave the secret knock. Paulo flung open the door and Gordon darted in before the parents in line could stop him.

"Hey!" shouted one man.

"I was here first!" insisted another, but it was too late. Gordon had locked the door behind him. Taking his seat beside me, Paulo grinned and said, "Look at that line of parents. This is great!" Several more parents had joined the unmoving line. Our plan was really working. A full five minutes passed and Gordon still had not emerged from the washroom. Parents rocked desperately from foot to foot, and several began to pound on the door.

"Hurry up in there!" one man shouted. Paulo and I tried to contain our laughter, and then out of the corner of my eye, I saw our teacher, Mrs. Hoagsbrith, rise from her seat and make her way to the back of the bus. Hearing the commotion, she had come to investigate. She worked her way to the front of the line and asked what the problem was. "Oh, some kid's in there tying up the washroom," said one mother.

"And we *really* have to go!" said another parent, a look of desperation on his face. Mrs. Hoagsbrith knocked sharply on the door.

"Who's in there?" she demanded.

"Gordon," came the reply.

"*Gordon?* I should have known. Now you get out right now!"

Wanting to stall our teacher for a few more minutes, Gordon decided to *really* play it up. "I can't come out yet. Just give me another minute, please." And then it happened. Figuring he could stall our teacher even longer, Gordon decided to let out one of his trademark farts. He made groaning sounds as he strained, and then in a final effort, he let out a loud fart. Unfortunately for Gordon, he had tried *too* hard, and he suddenly found himself with his pants full of what is known in polite company as Number

Two. As Paulo and I watched, the door to the washroom slowly opened and Gordon came out. The first parent in line rushed in and slammed the door behind her. Gordon walked slowly down the aisle. He sat down in the seat next to Paulo and me.

"What's wrong with you?" I asked, noting the strange look on Gordon's face. "Your plan worked brilliantly. You should have seen the looks on those parents' faces. I mean, they were desperate to go."

Gordon leaned across the aisle and whispered what had happened to Paulo and me. My jaw dropped open in surprise.

Now fortunately the bus drive had seen the long line-up for the washroom and decided to pull off the road at the nearest rest stop to let everyone use the washrooms. Parents charged off the bus and headed quickly inside. Gordon, Paulo and I were the last ones off the bus.

We headed straight for the souvenir shop at the rest stop, but to our dismay, several other kids from our class were already there. Not wanting anyone to know what had happened, Gordon pretended he was browsing. He picked up a really cool t-shirt and then he found a pair of sweat pants that almost perfectly matched the ones he was wearing. He took both items up to the cash register and placed them on the counter. The cashier was a real old lady. She slowly rung in Gordon's purchases and said, "That'll be forty-five dollars."

"Oh, I don't have that much money," replied Gordon. "Just the sweatpants, please," he said quietly.

"What?" said the old lady.

"Just the sweatpants," repeated Gordon a little louder, glancing around to make sure none of the other kids in our class were watching. He quickly paid the lady, grabbed the bag off the counter and the three of us ran to the bus which was just getting ready to leave. As the bus pulled onto the highway, Gordon headed straight for the washroom and locked himself inside. He quickly removed his sweatpants and underwear and looked around for a place to hide them. Finding nowhere suitable, he opened the tiny washroom window and flung the dirty clothes out of the bus. He closed the window, reached into the bag and pulled out *just the t-shirt*!

Chapter 9

Paint Ball Disaster

It was the end of June and there were only three days left of school! Shortly after nine o'clock, our principal, Mr. Evans, announced that he was calling a surprise assembly and told each class to make their way quietly to the gym.   When everyone had arrived and settled down, Mr. Evans got up on the stage and told us that he had some very good news.

"This school is being torn down next week and completely destroyed." Instantly, every kid in the gym leapt to their feet and began to cheer, scream and dance around. Mr. Evans roared into the microphone, "THAT IS *NOT* THE GOOD NEWS! SIT DOWN!!"

After we had settled down, he began again. "The *good* news is that a brand new modern school has been secretly under construction across town for the last six months and will be ready for September!" This was met by silence from the kids and a few surprised "oh's" from some of the teachers. Mr. Evans continued. "This new school has a brand new staff parking lot with extra-wide spaces and no potholes. It has a modern staff room with not one, but *two* top-of-the-line dishwashers. There are reclining chairs, and for those teachers who really want to relax during their prep time, I mean *recess break*, there are two heated massage chairs. There is an outdoor patio just off the staff room on the opposite side from the playground. Double doors from the patio lead to a fully-equipped Staff Wellness Centre. There is a staff workroom complete with state-of-the-art computers, tablets, and wi-fi that actually works." Suddenly, every teacher in the gym leapt to their feet and began cheering, screaming and dancing while the students sat silently watching, their expressions clearly stating *this isn't fair!*

When the teachers finally calmed down, Mr. Evans said, "I know what you kids are all thinking: *What about the students? What do we get out of this?* Well, every classroom will be equipped with not one, but two extra wide chalkboards. There will be extra hooks in the cloakrooms, and all of the toilets will flush!" Dead silence. "And I've saved the best for last." Mr. Evans paused for dramatic effect. "Since they are tearing this old, worn-out building down, I see no reason why we can't celebrate in some manner. I talked it over with the Parent Council, and they agreed that we should say good-bye to Danglemore Public School with a school-wide *paint-ball competition* on the last day of school! Class against class, and the teachers against all of you students! If the teachers win, they will each get one extra paid week of holidays, and if one of the classes wins, they will get an entire year of no homework!" The gym went wild!!

* * * * *

The last day of school arrived – the last day *ever* for Danglemore Public School. Every class had worked out their secret strategies. Parents were on hand to help the younger students get dressed in their helmets, goggles,

76

neck protectors and other protective gear. The grade 8 students, who would be going on to high school next year and had no reason to join in the competition, acted as referees. The baseball diamond was designated as the out-of-action area, where students and teachers would go when they were eliminated from play.

When the 9 am bell rang, every student and teacher was raring to go. It was every class for itself, and all the classes against the teachers!

Gordon had worked out our room's strategy, and it was pure genius. Our plan was to lock our classroom door and remain inside, conserving our energy and our paintball rations. We would let the rest of the school fight it out until there was only one class or the teachers left, and then, when they were low on ammo and worn out, we would burst out of our room and take them on. I closed my eyes and dreamed about a year with no homework.

A siren rang, signaling the beginning of the battle. From the safety of our classroom, we could hear the shouts and laughter and screams of delight as kids battled it out in the hallways. From our windows, we watched as entire classes were defeated and herded outside to the out-of-action area. As expected, the primary kids went first, followed by the middle grades, who fought a tough fight considering they were outnumbered and outpowered by the older students and the teachers. Within an hour, it began to get quiet in the school. Judging from the number of students in the out-of-action area, there were only two groups left besides our class – the teachers, and the grade 7s.

Suddenly, there was loud banging on the door. "We know you're in there!" came the voice of a grade 7 boy. "Come out and fight!" He peppered our classroom door with paint.

"Great plan, Gordon!" I said. "Now we're trapped! How are we supposed to get out the door without getting slaughtered?"

"Quick!" said Gordon. "Everyone follow me!" Using our gym clothes, Gordon had already made a long rope out of shorts and t-shirts which he tied to the teacher's heavy wooden desk. He opened a window and flung the loose end outside. "Climb down the rope!" he ordered. No one moved. There was more sharp banging on the door. "Open up or we'll bust the door down!" We instantly leapt into action, rappelling down the outside of the school like we were fresh out of army boot camp.

"Now what?" I asked Gordon. "As soon as they break into our classroom, they'll follow us down!"

"Then we'll just have to go back up!" yelled Gordon, and he raced back into the building and led us to the custodian's room, where a ladder led to the roof of the school. We no sooner made it to the roof when the grade 7s burst into our classroom, randomly spraying paintballs at everything in the room. When they discovered our rope, they quickly started climbing out of the window after us. Suddenly, from around the corner of the building, ten teachers leapt out and sprayed the students who clung to the rope. In 30 seconds it was all over. The grade 7s had been eliminated! The teachers began to cheer and clap each other on the back.

"Whoo-hoo! An extra week of paid vacation!" they cried.

"Not so fast," came the voice of Mrs. Hoagsbrith. "Are you forgetting that *my* class is still somewhere out here?" Thirty heads swiveled around the playground searching for us. "Up there!" cried our gym teacher, pointing to the roof. Thirty pairs of eyes trained themselves on the roof.

It was now us against the teachers…

Suddenly, a whistle sounded shrilly and from the parking lot, people in full paintball gear began pouring out of vans and cars and came trotting single-file to the playground where they joined the teachers.

"Who are they?" said Paulo, as the rest of our class looked on in fear.

"The teachers brought in reinforcements!" said Gordon in disbelief.

"That's right!" shouted Mr. Evans, in obvious delight. "Once word got out about our little paint-ball battle, every supply teacher your class has ever had *begged* us to let them join our team!"

"We're doomed!" I whispered.

"We need a new plan," said Gordon. "Let me think…"

"Well, hurry up," said Paulo. "The sun is broiling up here and I'm dying of thirst."

"Yeah," agreed several kids. "We won't have any strength left to fight if we don't get some water soon."

A group of girls volunteered to climb down into the building and bring us back some bottled water.

"Be careful," cautioned Gordon. "We'll need every single person to fight off all those teachers, so don't get Caught. And hurry back!" Six girls silently slipped down the ladder and back into the building.

"Wow!" breathed one girl. "Look at this mess!" Every inch of the walls, floors and ceilings was splattered in brightly coloured paint. Doors, windows and water fountains were coated. Even the books in the library and the computers in the lab were dripping with paint.

Reaching the staff room, the girls grabbed as many water bottles as they could find, and just as they were about to run back to the custodian's room and climb onto the roof, they heard someone ringing the front door buzzer. It was a mailwoman, balancing a large, awkward box.

"Just a second," said one of the girls, and she ran to let the struggling woman into the building. The minute the door was opened, the mailwoman reached into her box, pulled out a paint-gun, and splattered five of the girls from head to toe with bright orange paint! "Gotcha!!" she cried. "That's for being the worst class I ever had to supply in."

Only one girl managed to get away. She dashed back up to the roof and immediately reported what had happened.

"An ambush!" said Gordon between clenched teeth. "A supply teacher disguised as a mailwoman! What a dirty trick!! And why didn't I think of it? Well, we won't fall for that again! Come on, everyone! Let's go charge at these teachers!!"

As we were climbing down the ladder, we could hear a police siren in the distance getting closer and closer. Just as we hit the ground and ran outside, a police car pulled into the parking lot, lights flashing and sirens blaring. Out jumped two police officers.

"HA!" yelled Gordon. "They're not going to fool us again. Of all the low-down, dirty tricks. Fake cops!! It's another ambush! Take aim, everyone! *FIRE!!*" Dutifully we opened up on the officers, coating them from head to foot with paint. When the so-called police officers were completely covered in purple paint, we opened up on their cruiser.

"STOP! *STOP!*" cried Mr. Evans, but we paid no attention. Not until every inch of the cruiser was covered in purple paint did we stop, and then we turned our paint guns towards our teachers.

That's funny, I thought. *All of the teachers have laid their paint guns down. And why is Mr. Evans holding his head in his hands and moaning like that?* And then it happened. The fake police officers began yelling and shaking their handcuffs in the direction of Mr. Evans. Suddenly, they didn't sound very much like supply teachers dressed up like police officers. They sounded very much like *real* police officers! *Real police officers that we had just covered from head to toe in purple paint!!*

"Wow!" breathed Gordon. "Let's do the right thing and surrender and give Mr. Evans the opportunity to take full responsibility for this mess." We quietly joined the rest of the students in the out-of-action area.

"I can't wait to hear your explanation, and it had better be good," said one of the officers as purple paint dripped from his head and ran down his collar. "But we really just came by to tell you that there has been an accident at the site of the new school. It burned down to the ground this morning, and Danglemore Public School won't be torn down after all."

I don't know who was more shocked, the teachers or the kids. We all turned to look at our school, which was covered in a rainbow of paint splatters inside and out. Everywhere you looked, there was paint - on the playground equipment, the basketball hoops, the bike racks, the trees, the windows, the bricks, even the school sign. Inside, things were far worse. Every desk, chair, wall and ceiling was coated in paint. Paint dripped from the lights. Even the toilets were polka-dotted with paint.

"Oh, by the way," said one of the officers. "I'll bet it's going to take *weeks* to clean our uniforms and cruiser, to say nothing of *your school*. You'd all better get busy. I guess there'll be no vacation for *anyone* this summer!"